Pip hurried along the cliff.

He was careful not to get too close to the edge. The wind was blowing strong enough to make his eyes water. If his slicker filled with air, Pip knew he could blow away like a kite.

Suddenly, a gust of wind smacked him in the face. He turned his back, and when he did, he saw something move.

Pip squinted his eyes. Someone wearing a black rain slicker was walking about a hundred yards behind him. Whoever it was had the hood up. Pip couldn't see a face under the hood. Just a dark hole.

Pip felt the hair on his neck stand straight up. He broke out in a rash of goose bumps.

Someone was following him!

This book is dedicated to Mike Pardue

Text copyright © 1996 by Ron Roy.
Illustrations copyright © 1996 by Elizabeth Wolf.

All rights reserved under International and Pan-American Copyright Conventions.
Published in the United States by Random House, Inc., New York, and
simultaneously in Canada by Random House of Canada Limited, Toronto.

http://www.randomhouse.com/

Library of Congress Cataloging-in-Publication Data
Roy, Ron
Someone is following Pip Ramsey / by Ron Roy ; illustrated by Elizabeth Wolf.
  p. cm.
"A Stepping Stone book."
SUMMARY: At the start of his family's vacation on the coast of Maine, nine-year-old
Pip Ramsey buys an old Russian nesting doll at a yard sale and is soon certain that
someone is extremely interested in getting the doll from him.
ISBN 0-679-87498-4 (pbk.) — ISBN 0-679-97498-9 (lib. bdg.)
[1. Dolls—Fiction. 2. Vacations—Fiction.] I. Wolf, Elizabeth, ill. II. Title.
PZ7.R8139So 1996 [Fic]—dc20 95-26235

Printed in the United States of America 10 9 8 7 6 5 4 3 2 1

Someone Is Following Pip Ramsey

by Ron Roy

illustrated by Elizabeth Wolf

A STEPPING STONE BOOK

Random House 🏠 New York

1

Pip Ramsey was tired of being squished in with the suitcases and sleeping bags. Twice he'd banged his head on the food cooler, and now he had a cramp in his leg.

"Why do I always have to ride back here?" he asked for about the hundredth time. "Why can't Mike?"

"Because you're such a little pipsqueak you fit back there," his brother informed him. "Now quit squeaking, Squeaky."

Pip didn't mind being called Pip. He even kind of liked the nickname. But lately Mike had started calling him Squeak, Squeaky, and Squeaker. Could he help it if he was the shortest fourth-grader in the world?

"Stop!" Pip's mother shouted. "A yard sale!"

His father pulled up the station wagon next to a sign sticking out of a clump of weeds. The sign said: MOVING SALE TODAY— LOTS OF GOOD STUFF!

Mike's head popped up. "Do we have to, Mom? Can't we just get to the cottage? I need a bathroom right now!"

His mother turned around. "Mike, I'm sure there's a bathroom at that gas station across the road. We'll just be here a few minutes. I promise!"

Pip got up on his knees and looked through the window. He saw a row of tables set up in a dusty farmyard. People were wandering around looking at furniture and other items for sale.

Pip liked old stuff. His parents owned an antiques shop in Boston, and he grew up playing with other people's junk.

Pip's dad parked the station wagon behind a line of pickup trucks and cars. He got out and opened the rear doors. "Stretch your legs, you guys."

"It's about time!" Mike sprinted for the gas station.

Pip hopped out and looked around. "How long can we stay?"

His mother checked her watch. "Come looking for us in about fifteen minutes, okay?"

Pip checked his own watch. Then he took off into the crowd.

He saw a kid about his age standing behind a table loaded with old toys. The boy's dark hair hung in his eyes. His flannel shirt looked as though it had been worn by a few other people before it got to him.

Pip walked over to the table. He picked up a truck that was missing one wheel. "How much is this?"

The boy flicked some hair out of his eyes. "Fifty cents, I guess."

Pip set the truck down and picked up a G.I. Joe with only one arm.

"That's fifty cents, too."

"But it's broken!" said Pip.

"Everything around here is broken," the boy told him.

A man with the same dark hair and eyes as the boy walked out of the barn. He plunked a box down on the table. "Here's a few more toys, son."

Pip watched the boy unpack the box. He took out a split baseball, a plastic pail with no handle, and a worn wooden doll painted to look like a farmer boy.

Pip picked up the doll. It was about ten inches tall, with a round body and a flat bottom. The arms, legs, face, and clothes were painted on the wood. Most of the paint was faded or chipped away.

"It's hollow," the boy said. "Pull the top off."

Pip pulled and the doll came apart at the waist. Inside he found another farmer boy, smaller than the first one. Pip pulled apart the second doll and found a third, even smaller doll inside. He tried to pull apart the third doll, but it didn't open.

Pip rubbed his hands over the smooth, worn wood. He liked the way the painted faces smiled, as if they knew a secret.

"What'll you take for this?" he asked.

"How about a dollar?" said the boy.

"Okay, but I have to get the money from my mother." Pip put the three dolls back together. "Can I show it to her?"

The boy shrugged. "Sure."

Pip went looking for his mother. He found her standing with some other people at a table covered with books, pictures, and records.

Pip tugged his mother's sleeve. "Mom, can I buy this? It's neat. Look." He pulled the doll apart. "It's only a dollar."

"Just let me write a check first," she said. "Daddy and I found some wonderful record albums for the shop."

His mother signed the check and handed it to a woman standing behind the table.

The woman read the check carefully. "Thank you, Mrs. Ramsey. You're not from Ogunquit?"

Pip's mother shook her head. "Boston. We're renting the Pardues' cottage out by the cliffs. It's our third year here."

Pip tugged his mother's sleeve again.

"Mom, can I have the dollar?"

"That doll came over from Russia with my husband's great-aunt a long time ago," the woman told Pip.

"It's beautiful," Pip's mother said, handing him a dollar. "Meet us at the car in five minutes, honey."

Pip ran back to the boy's table and gave him the dollar.

The boy jammed the dollar into his pocket. "Do you live around here?"

"Just for the summer," Pip told him. "I live in Massachusetts the rest of the year. Do you know Davey Donaldson?"

The boy shook his head. "I don't know very many people. We haven't lived here that long, and now we have to move again. As soon as my folks can sell this place."

The boy glanced over his shoulder at the farmhouse. Then he looked back at Pip. "My name's Matt. What's yours?"

"Brad Ramsey," Pip said. "But everyone calls me Pip."

"That's because he's such a pipsqueak,"

Mike said, coming up behind Pip. "Come on, we're leaving."

Pip waved good-bye to Matt and headed back toward the car, tossing his doll in the air. Mike was lugging something that looked like half a bicycle.

"What's that thing?" asked Pip.

"It's a unicycle. Watch an expert." Mike stood the unicycle on the ground and climbed onto the seat. He and the unicycle fell over.

Pip laughed. "Neat trick, Mike. Can you do it again?"

Mike brushed off his jeans. "Shut up, Squeaker. At least I didn't buy a dumb doll."

"It's a magic genie," Pip said. "When I rub his stomach, he grants me a wish."

He rubbed the doll and grinned at his brother. "Guess what I'm wishing for?"

"I give up, Squeak."

"A million dollars. Then I'll make you my slave. You'll have to wait on me forever until I die."

Mike laughed. "I like that last part."

2

Mike and Pip unloaded the car while their parents unlocked the cottage and opened the windows.

Pip lugged his sleeping bag and duffel bag upstairs to his room. He made a sign that said DO NOT ENTER!!! He hung the sign on the outside of his door and shut it.

Then he unpacked his stuff. He stood his books neatly on a shelf. He placed his dinosaurs in a row, from shortest to tallest. He stacked his games on a chest next to his bed.

He was starting to unpack his clothes when he heard a knock. "It's Mom."

"Enter!" Pip said. His mother walked in and raised his window as high as it would go.

"Isn't this view something? Boats, sea-gulls, rocks, just like a Norman Rockwell painting." His mother took a deep breath. "And the smell of pine trees and salt water! How I love this place!"

Pip found his cut-off jeans. "You say that every year, Mom."

"And I mean it every year."

"I'm going over to see Davey, okay?" said Pip.

"Okay, but please be back by five-fifteen. We're having an early supper. Then it's bed for everyone."

A minute later Pip was jogging along the cliff path. Davey's house was about half a mile away. Like the Pardues' cottage, it had been built near the cliff, with a view of the Maine seacoast.

He followed the cliff path, pretending he was an Ogunquit Indian boy. He kept his eyes peeled for arrowheads the whole way.

Davey's sister, Lindsay, came to the door when Pip knocked. Lindsay was thirteen, the same age as Mike. Her face was tan and her hair was as black as crow feathers. She didn't look anything like her little brother. Davey had red hair and freckles.

"Pip, you've gotten so tall!" She mussed his hair and grinned at him.

Pip knew he hadn't grown an inch since last summer. Lindsay was just trying to make him feel good. He blushed. "Where's Davey?"

"Here I am!" Davey shot through the screen door. A black puppy came with him, dragging a white sock.

Davey Donaldson was nine, Pip's age. They'd been pals since Pip's first summer in Ogunquit.

Davey and Pip sat on the porch steps and watched the puppy play with the sock.

"We just got him," Davey told Pip. "His name's Jason."

Davey grabbed the sock from Jason. "Watch this." He let Jason sniff the sock. Then he hid it under a big seashell on the porch. "Where's your sock, boy? Jason, find the sock!"

Jason went right for the shell. He tipped

it over with his nose and grabbed the sock with his teeth.

"Now hide the sock, Jason. Hide Lindsay's smelly old sock!"

Jason dug a hole near the porch and buried the sock.

"I'm teaching him to steal Lindsay's stuff," Davey explained. "It drives her crazy. Then I tell her I'll find it if she gives me a reward."

Lindsay yelled from inside. "Come and wash up, Davey."

"I have to go," said Davey. "Do you want to come over tomorrow? We can catch crabs for my aquarium."

"Okay," said Pip. They gave each other a high five.

Pip headed back along the cliff. Halfway home he stopped to watch the waves crash against the rocks.

Suddenly the back of his neck felt tingly, the way it did when he watched scary movies. He turned around to see if anyone was behind him. But there was no one on the path or on the beach below the cliff.

Goose bumps popped out on Pip's arms. He knew he was being dumb. But he ran home anyway, still feeling goose bumps all over.

3

Pip was getting dressed the next morning when the phone rang.

"Will somebody please answer the phone!" his mother yelled from somewhere in the house.

Pip ran down the hall to answer it. "Hello, Ramsey residence."

"Is this the young man who bought the doll at the yard sale yesterday?"

"This is him," Pip said. "Who's this?"

It was a woman's voice on the line. A voice Pip didn't recognize.

"Will you sell me the doll?" the voice went on. "I collect Russian dolls."

"Who is this?" Pip asked again. Something about this call made him feel weird.

"I'll give you twenty dollars," the voice said.

Pip thought about what he could buy for twenty dollars. But he liked the doll.

"No thanks," he said. "Who is this, anyway?"

He heard a click as the caller hung up. Pip shrugged and went to his room to finish getting dressed.

A few minutes later he went downstairs to eat breakfast with his family.

"Who was that on the phone?" his mother asked.

Pip spread some strawberry jam on his pancakes. "Someone wants to buy that doll I bought yesterday." He looked at his brother. "They offered me twenty bucks!"

Mike snorted. "In your dreams. Twenty dollars for a stupid little doll? Don't lie, Pip."

Pip's father looked up from his newspaper. "Someone offered you money over the phone? Did they say who it was?"

Pip shook his head. "Nope. I asked, but they hung up." He glared at Mike. "And I'm not lying."

Mike stretched and yawned. "Dad, can I buy a motorbike?"

His father shook his head. "When you're sixteen, we'll talk. Until then you'll walk."

"Dad's a poet and doesn't know it," Pip said. "No bike for Mike!"

Mike stuck out his tongue. "Very funny, Squeak."

"What's the schedule today, fellas?" their father asked. "Big plans?"

Mike stopped shoveling in his pancakes. "Me and Chuck are going fishing at his uncle's house."

"I'm going over to Davey's," Pip said around a mouthful of pancake.

"Don't talk with your mouth full," Mike said. "It's disgusting!"

Pip grinned at his brother with his mouth wide open.

His father poured himself more coffee. "Mom and I might pop into a few yard sales this morning."

"We'll be home for lunch," Pip's mother said. "I'd like you both back here by noon, please."

Pip ran upstairs to get his backpack. He threw in the wooden doll. Back in the kitchen, he grabbed an apple and some crackers and tossed them in, too. Then he took off for Davey's house.

Lindsay was reading on a blanket. "Hi, Pip. Davey's out back." She grinned. "You've got jam on your nose."

Pip wiped his nose with the back of his hand. "We're gonna catch some crabs today."

"I know. Davey's been lugging water for his aquarium. Have fun!"

Pip walked around to the back of the house. Davey was pouring a pail of water into the aquarium. Jason was digging a hole in the dirt.

"Hi," Davey said. "Let's go while the tide's out." He whistled. "Come on, Jason. Beach!"

Pip and Davey walked down to the beach. Jason ran ahead through the sand dunes and tall beach grass, trying to catch grasshoppers.

Pip stopped to pick up a seashell. He put it in his pack and ran to catch up with Davey.

"Where are those crabs?" he asked.

"Follow me!" Davey raced toward some seaweed-covered rocks near the water. A tide pool had collected between them. Nearby, shorebirds were searching for food. Jason barked and ran toward the birds.

Pip pulled off his sneakers and left them with his pack. He knelt next to Davey over the tide pool. Tiny silver fish darted around the pool when the boys' shadows fell on the water. A few green crabs scurried for cover.

Davey dropped his net into the water and pulled out a green crab the size of a Ritz cracker. "I put one of these in Lindsay's bed once."

Pip grinned. "What happened?"

"She squealed to Mom. I had to change her bed and wash her sheets."

They caught some more crabs and

dropped them into Davey's pail. Jason came back and they played monkey-in-the-middle with one of Pip's sneakers.

"I'm getting hungry," Pip said. He sat down on a large rock and put his sneakers back on. Then he opened his backpack. He showed Davey the shell he'd picked up in the dunes.

"So? I've got a million of those."

"I'm collecting these round ones," Pip explained. "When I get enough, I'm making my mom a necklace."

Pip took the crackers out of his pack. He made two small piles on his knees, one for himself and one for Davey. Jason started whining, so they each fed him a cracker.

"Look." Pip pulled the doll out of the pack. "I bought this at a yard sale yesterday." He twisted the doll's top off and showed Davey the second doll inside.

"Excellent!" Davey pulled out the second doll and gave the top a twist. The third doll fell out. He tried to pull it apart, but nothing happened.

Pip dropped his shell inside the second

doll for safekeeping. "That little one doesn't open," he said. "There's no crack in it. Guess what, though? Someone called me this morning. They asked if they could buy the doll for twenty dollars."

Davey ate another cracker. "Twenty bucks! Are you gonna sell it?"

Before Pip could answer, Jason lunged for the smallest doll. In a second he was racing down the beach with the doll in his mouth.

4

"Jason! Bad dog! Come back!" yelled Davey.

Pip and Davey chased Jason through the sand dunes until they lost sight of him. They yelled and whistled, but it was no use.

Pip kicked a clump of seaweed. "Why'd you let your dumb dog take my doll?"

"I didn't *let* him take anything."

They were red-faced and puffing as they walked back to the rocks.

"He just grabbed it," said Davey. "But he'll probably bring it home. That's where he buries all his stuff."

"He better!" Pip threw the other two dolls into his backpack and started walking

toward Davey's house. He didn't even offer
to help Davey carry the pail of crabs.

On his porch, Davey emptied the pail
into the aquarium. "Sorry about the doll," he
mumbled.

Pip watched the crabs scurry toward the
bottom of the aquarium. "Sorry I got mad. I
guess it wasn't your fault. You really think
Jason will bring it back?"

"Probably. He buries stuff all over the
yard."

While Pip and Davey were filling the
aquarium with rocks and shells, Jason showed
up. Without the doll.

"Bad dog!" Davey yelled.

Lindsay spoke through the screen door.
"Who wants a glass of lemonade?"

The boys trooped inside. They drank two
glasses of lemonade apiece.

"Davey, don't forget we have to meet
Mom in town," said Lindsay. "Please fill your
dog's water bowl and be ready in five minutes."

Davey and Pip went out on the porch.

Davey used the hose to give Jason some fresh water.

"That's funny," Pip said. "My pack's gone. It was right here next to the aquarium."

"Maybe you left it down at the beach," said Davey.

"I know I brought it up here, Davey. You carried the pail and I carried my pack."

"How could it just disappear?"

"What disappeared?" Lindsay asked, looking through the screen door.

"Someone snitched Pip's backpack right off the porch!" Davey told his sister.

"Calm down, Davey. Nobody stole anything." Lindsay glanced around the backyard. "Maybe Jason dragged it off somewhere. He's famous for stealing things."

Pip walked around one side of the house, looking in all the bushes. Davey and Lindsay went around the other side. They found a tennis ball and one of Lindsay's sneakers, but no backpack and no little wooden doll.

"We better get going. Sorry, Pip," said Lindsay.

"I'll look some more when I get home," Davey promised.

Pip walked home slowly along the cliff path. He was thinking.

Maybe Jason buried the doll. But would he bury my pack, too?

A few minutes later he reached the Pardue cottage. Mike and Chuck were back from fishing. They were in the yard, practicing on Mike's unicycle.

"Hey, Squeak," said Mike.

Pip didn't answer. He went inside and told his mother about his missing backpack.

"I think someone stole it," he said.

His mother raised her eyebrows. "Someone stole your backpack right off Davey's porch? Did you maybe leave it at the beach?"

Pip shook his head. "Mom, I know what I did. I remember putting it next to the aquarium."

"Are you sure, honey?"

"I'm not lying, Mom!" said Pip.

"No one thinks you're lying, it's just—"

"Mike thinks I lie."

His mother opened the refrigerator door. She stared inside for a minute. "I'm sure your pack will turn up," she said. "It has to be somewhere."

When Pip's father got home, they all ate tuna sandwiches on the porch. Chuck and Mike were sweaty from riding the unicycle.

"How about ice cream in town and a little miniature golf?" Pip's father suggested.

They all piled into the station wagon. Pip had to sit in the back, as usual.

When they got to Gopher Golf, they split into teams—Mike and Chuck against Pip and his parents. Each team won two games.

"Let's play a tiebreaker," said Mike.

His father shook his head. "Nope. Let's just wonder who the champions would be."

They dropped Chuck off at his house and drove back to the cottage. The minute Pip walked into his room, he knew something was wrong.

His dinosaurs weren't lined up by size anymore. And one of his drawers was sticking out. Pip crossed the hall to Mike's room.

"Have you been in my room?" he challenged his brother.

"No," said Mike.

"Then why are my dinosaurs all messed up?" asked Pip.

"How do I know? I was with you at Gopher Golf, remember? So how could I be in your room at the same time?"

"Someone was," Pip said. "And I'm not lying."

Mike pulled off his T-shirt. "First *someone* stole your backpack. Now *someone* is playing with your little toys. Boy, are you paranoid!"

"I'm not paranoid!" Pip yelled. He went back to his room and slammed the door.

5

Pip was sound asleep the next morning when someone touched his shoulder. He jumped and opened his eyes. His father was bending over him.

"Good morning, sleepyhead. Did I scare you?"

"I dreamed some robbers came and took a bunch of stuff from our house," Pip said. "I thought you were them."

Pip sat up and told his father about finding his dinosaurs disturbed the night before.

"And my dresser drawers were sticking out a little," Pip said. "I always push them in."

"Maybe your brother did it."

32

Pip shook his head. "I asked him. He called me paranoid."

Pip's father laughed. "Brothers, huh? I'm cooking eggs. Hurry up and get dressed."

Pip dressed and hurried downstairs. His father had made scrambled eggs hard, the way Pip liked them. His mother was spreading cream cheese on toasted bagels.

Mike came in, yawning. "What's for breakfast?"

"The early birds get the worms," his father said.

Mike grinned and made a gaggy face. "You guys are eating worms?"

Pip's father put a bagel on a plate for Mike. "Were you in Pip's room yesterday?"

Mike sat down and shook his head. "I told him it wasn't me, Dad."

"Well, I was in there a few times to put clothes away," Pip's mother said.

Pip told his mother about the dinosaurs.

"Maybe we should start locking the doors," Pip's father said.

"Maybe Pip should stop making up stories," said Mike, chomping on his bagel.

Pip made a face at his brother.

After breakfast Pip called Davey's house, but no one answered. He wanted to ask Davey if he had found the doll or his backpack. He dialed a few more times, then gave up.

The sky grew darker, and by noon thick clouds promised rain. Pip's mother brought out the Monopoly board and a pitcher of iced tea.

While they were counting out the money, a pickup truck pulled into the driveway. Pip recognized the woman from the yard sale. It was Matt's mother.

Pip's mother waved. "Hi. Come on up and have some iced tea with us."

"I don't want to disturb you," Matt's mother said. She climbed the porch steps.

Mike excused himself and Pip's father offered her the empty chair. "I'm sorry, but I don't remember your name," he said.

"I'm Joan Donavich," she said. Then she looked right at Pip. "I came to buy the doll back."

Pip didn't get a chance to tell her that he didn't have the doll anymore.

"My husband wants it," she went on. "His great-aunt brought the doll here from Russia when she was a little girl. He wants us to keep it in the family."

She pulled some money out of her pocket. "He was upset that Matthew sold it. We'll pay for it, of course."

"But I don't have the doll anymore," Pip said. He explained how Jason stole the littlest doll. Then he told her about the missing backpack with the other two parts of the doll inside.

Matt's mother looked upset. "It's gone? But we…can you find it?"

"Pip, why don't you and Davey make a real effort to find the dolls," his father said. "I'm willing to bet they'll turn up somewhere around his house."

Matt's mother stood up. "Thank you. We'll buy the doll back if you find it."

"Of course we won't ask you to pay for your own doll," Pip's mother said. "When it shows up, we'll gladly give it back."

In his room later, Pip watched the lightning zigzag out of the black clouds. He thought about what Matt's mother told them. It didn't make sense.

He remembered Matt's father handing Matt a box of toys to sell. The doll was right on top. If he wanted to keep the doll in the family, why did he let Matt sell it?

Thunder boomed over the house. Pip shivered.

Someone's lying, he thought. *And it isn't me.*

6

The next morning, when Pip looked out his window, he saw rain. It rained while he got dressed and it was still pouring when he called Davey.

"Hi, it's Pip. Dumb weather, huh?"

"Yeah. Guess what? I found your pack."

"You did! Where was it?"

"In the field between our house and the Fletchers'. Jason must have dragged it over there."

"Was my doll in it?"

"Yup."

So he had half of the doll back. Well, two-thirds. Now all he had to do was find the part that Jason stole and Matt's mother would be happy.

Except that Pip didn't want to give the doll to Matt's parents. There was something strange going on. Pip knew Matt's mother hadn't told the truth last night. But why would she lie?

"Hey, you still there?" Davey said.

Pip had almost forgotten Davey. "I'm coming over," he said.

Pip's mother made him eat breakfast. She insisted that he wear his rain slicker. She made him promise not to play near the cliffs. "And tell Lindsay thank you for watching you guys."

Out the door finally, Pip hurried along the cliff. He was careful not to get too close to the edge. The wind was blowing strong enough to make his eyes water. If his slicker filled with air, Pip knew he could blow away like a kite.

Suddenly, a gust of wind smacked him in the face. He turned his back, and when he did, he saw something move.

Pip squinted his eyes. Someone wearing a

black rain slicker was walking about a hundred yards behind him. Whoever it was had the hood up. Pip couldn't see a face under the hood. Just a dark hole.

Pip felt the hair on his neck stand straight up. He broke out in a rash of goose bumps. Someone was following him!

Pip started running. He didn't dare look back. His heart was beating so loud he couldn't have heard footsteps behind him, anyway.

A minute later Pip banged on Davey's back door. He looked over his shoulder. He saw only wet rocks and bushes and trees. Nobody in a black slicker.

Dumb, he said to himself. Probably just some guy out taking a walk. Or a bird watcher. He felt foolish.

Davey opened the door and Pip slipped inside.

"Hi," Davey said.

Pip hung his dripping slicker on the doorknob. "Where's my backpack?"

"Upstairs."

They went to Davey's bedroom. The pack was on his bed. Pip pulled out the doll.

"Has Jason brought back the other one yet?"

Davey shook his head. "We can look, though. There's a lot of stuff buried in this yard."

Pip twisted the doll apart and took out the second one. He looked inside all four pieces. "That's funny. It's gone."

"What's gone?"

"Remember that shell I found yesterday? I put it inside this doll so I wouldn't lose it." He showed Davey the empty halves. "It isn't here."

"What do you mean?"

"The shell is gone, Davey," said Pip.

"What's the big deal about a shell?"

"I don't *care* about the shell," Pip said. "I'm just saying that Jason couldn't have taken my pack. How could a puppy open a doll, take a shell out, then put the doll back together again?"

"So if Jason didn't do it, who did?"

"I don't know, but I think something weird is going on," said Pip. "First I get a phone call and someone wants to buy the doll. Then my backpack disappears. And listen to this. We went to play miniature golf the other day. While we were gone, someone messed around in my room."

Davey's eyes opened wide. "Someone broke into your house?"

Pip nodded. "I know someone was in there. And now I think someone was following me on my way over here."

"Who'd want to follow you?"

Pip felt the goose bumps all over again. "That's what I want to know. But I saw someone behind me wearing a long black rain slicker. Weird, right?"

"Something else is weird," Davey said. "If someone stole your pack to get the doll, why is the doll still in the pack?"

Pip looked at the two big dolls on Davey's bed. "Maybe they want all three parts."

"What happens if we can't find the third one?"

Pip dropped the two dolls back into his pack. He slid the pack under the bed. "I don't know. My folks said I have to give the doll back to Matt's parents. Matt's mom told us they want to keep it in the family. But I don't believe her."

Pip looked out Davey's bedroom window. The wind was blowing rain against the glass. "Come on. Let's go ask Matt why his father really wants the doll back."

7

Davey borrowed Lindsay's ten-speed and Pip rode Davey's mountain bike. They pedaled toward Matt's farm, with Pip in the lead. Pip had his slicker hood up, but rain still blew into his face. His feet and legs got splashed from water slapping off his front tire.

Behind him, Davey was wearing his ski jacket and a red hunter's cap. Twice he yelled, "How much farther is this place? I'm soaked!"

When they rode into the dirt driveway, Matt's house and barn looked even gloomier than Pip remembered.

Davey jumped off his bike and stared.

"You sure they didn't move already? The place looks spooky."

Pip looked around the muddy yard. Then he noticed Matt standing near the barn, watching them.

Pip waved. "Come on," he said to Davey.

Matt was wearing high rubber boots and a black raincoat that was way too big for him. He was holding a smelly pail of garbage. He smiled when he recognized Pip. "Want to watch me feed the pigs? We got ten babies!"

Pip followed Matt through the mud. He was glad he didn't have Matt's job. He heard Davey behind him, squishing and slipping through the puddles.

Inside the pen, Pip saw two huge black-and-white pigs digging in the muck with their noses. A third one was flopped right in the mud. Ten muddy piglets were squished at her side, sucking like crazy.

Pip and Davey leaned on the top rail. "Neat!" Davey said. "Do you play with the babies?"

Matt shook his head. "My dad doesn't let

us make pets out of them. He'll sell the piglets as soon as they get bigger. All but the ones we eat."

The two adult pigs trotted over to the fence at the sound of Matt's voice. He dumped the garbage into their trough. They stuck their faces right in and started chomping. The sow feeding her babies didn't even look up.

Matt hung the bucket on a nail. "You guys want to come in and have a soda?"

"Sure." Pip looked toward the house. "Are your folks home?"

It would be pretty hard asking Matt why his mother had lied about the doll—if she lied—with her right there in the house.

Matt shook his head. "They're in town with my sisters."

They ran through the rain, splashing through the mud puddles. Matt left his boots on the back porch. Pip and Davey kicked off their wet sneakers.

Inside, the house looked more cheerful

than Pip expected. Yellow curtains hung at the windows. The wooden floor felt smooth under his damp socks.

Matt took three cans of soda from the refrigerator.

"Are you guys still moving?" Pip asked.

"Mom wants to stay here," Matt said. "She likes Maine. Dad does, too, but he says the land's too rocky for farming. He wants to move to Florida."

Pip made small circles on the table with his wet soda can. He thought Matt looked sad about moving.

"Your mom came to our house last night," he said.

"Yeah, I know. It's about that doll I sold you, right?"

Pip nodded. "She said your dad was mad at you for selling it and he wants it back."

Matt shook his head. "He wasn't mad. He just told Mom to get it back because he could sell it for a lot of money."

Pip stared at Matt. "Sell it? But your mom told us he wanted to keep it in the family. She said some old aunt brought it over from Russia."

Matt shrugged. "All I know is someone called my dad and offered him two hundred bucks for it."

Davey nearly choked. "Two hundred bucks for a doll?"

Pip felt like choking, too.

"Who called your dad?" Pip asked.

Matt shrugged. "Beats me. Dad just told my mom to try and get the doll back from you." He looked embarrassed. "I guess we need the money."

Pip wondered why Matt's mother didn't tell them the real reason her husband wanted the doll back.

He wondered if Matt's father had snuck into his bedroom to look for the doll. Did Matt's father follow him and Davey to the beach yesterday? Did he see them playing with the doll, then snatch the backpack off Davey's porch?

"So are you selling it back to us?" Matt asked.

"I only have the two biggest dolls," Pip said. "Davey's dog stole the little one and hid it somewhere."

Matt grinned. "He stole it?"

"He takes everything," Davey said. "Most of the stuff usually turns up again after a while."

"We're going to look for it today," Pip told Matt. "If we find it, my mom will call yours and you guys can have the doll back."

"Great," Matt said. "I'll tell my folks when they get home."

"The thing is," Pip said, "we might not be able to find the little one. Whoever called your father wants all three parts, don't they?"

Matt shrugged. "I don't know. Maybe they'll call again, and my dad can ask them."

Pip and Davey thanked Matt for the drinks and pulled on their muddy sneakers. The rain had stopped and the sun flashed brightly through the clouds.

They raced their bikes back to Davey's house. Munching on apples, they sat on the back porch. Pip made a plan.

"I'll take Jason back to the beach where he snitched the doll. I'll let him sniff one of the dolls from my pack. Then I'll let him take it, and I'll follow him. Maybe he'll lead me to where he hid the first one."

"What do I do?" Davey asked.

"You know all the places around here where he buries stuff, right? While I'm at the beach, you can dig up his holes."

"Jeez, why do I have to do the hard stuff? It's your doll."

Pip smacked his friend on the shoulder. "Yeah, and *your* dog stole it, don't forget. Come on, this won't take long."

8

Pip carried Jason back to the rocks where they'd eaten crackers two days before. He pulled the middle-size doll out of his pocket and let the puppy sniff it. Then he dropped the doll in the sand in front of Jason's nose. Jason grabbed it and bolted away.

"Good. Now I'm going to follow you, you little stealer!" Pip said. He ran after Jason, but the pup was too fast. Pip lost him in the dunes.

"Not so fast!" Pip yelled. He kicked the sand. Darn. If he couldn't keep up with Jason, how could he see where he took the doll?

Pip wandered among the dunes, calling Jason's name. The sand was too slippery and deep to leave puppy prints. He saw two little kids with plastic pails burying each other's legs.

"Did you guys see a black puppy run by here?"

The kids looked up. "He ran over our castle!" One of them poked his foot toward a crumbled sand building.

"I think he went that way," the other one said, pointing over the dunes toward Davey's house.

Pip took off running. When he got to Davey's backyard, he looked around. "Jason? Are you here, boy? Come on, Jason. Where are you?"

There was no sign of the puppy. "Great. Now he's got two dolls," Pip muttered. He looked for Davey, but he didn't see him, either.

Pip knocked on Davey's back door. "Davey, are you in there? Where the heck are you?"

No one answered. Pip sat down on the porch and put his head in his hands.

He heard a noise coming from under the porch. Pip jumped down and looked through a hole in the latticework. "You're in there, aren't you, boy?"

Pip saw Jason sprawled out in the dirt, staring back at him.

"Jason, be a good doggie. Come on out here, okay? Please?"

The puppy whined, but he didn't budge. Pip knew he'd have to crawl in after him, and the thought made him feel creepy. There were spiders in there, and who knew what else. Snakes hid in dark places, didn't they?

Pip got down on his belly and started to wiggle through the opening. A piece of wood caught on the waist of his shorts. He reached back and freed himself.

He felt spiderwebs stick to his face and eyelashes. The dirt was damp and cool on his hands and belly. He smelled something rotten and prayed he wasn't crawling into a skunk's living room.

Before his thoughts got any scarier, Pip squirmed over to Jason. The puppy welcomed him with a wet lick.

Pip patted Jason on the head. His eyes adjusted to the dark, and he saw Lindsay's white sock and a chewed-up Nerf football of Davey's.

And something else. Between Jason's front paws, Pip saw the wooden doll he'd just run off with.

"Good boy, Jason!" He pulled the doll away and shoved it into his back pocket.

"Now, where's the other one, boy? Is it here, too? Did you bring them both to the same place?" Pip felt around in the dirt, hoping to feel a smooth, hard lump. The only lumps he found were rocks and a few seashells.

Then he felt a patch of soft dirt. Pip started digging with both hands. He found the little doll buried a few inches down.

"Yes!" Pip shouted, and bumped his head on the underside of the porch. He stuck the doll into his front pocket. He rubbed Jason behind the ears and backed out from under the porch.

Pip stood up to brush himself off in the sun. A shadow fell over his shoulder.

Pip whipped around. A woman was standing there. She wore a long black rain slicker and sunglasses. She was smiling at Pip and holding a pink beach bag.

Pip felt goose bumps rising on his arms. "Who are you?"

"Never mind that," the woman said. "I want to buy that doll." She was pointing at the one sticking out of Pip's front pocket.

Pip recognized the voice. It was the woman who had offered him twenty dollars over the telephone.

"It's not for sale," he said. "I bought it and I'm keeping it."

"I know you bought it," the woman said. "I was at the yard sale. I simply want to buy the doll from you now. I collect Russian dolls." She pulled a small purse out of her bag.

Pip thought about running. He wasn't

supposed to talk to strangers. He took a step backward and felt the porch against his legs.

"You called me, right? Then when I wouldn't sell you the doll, you called Matt's father. You offered him two hundred dollars."

The woman waved her hand. "None of that is important," she said. She wasn't smiling as much now. "How much will you take for the doll?"

Pip inched his way to the right. "I can't sell it. My father says I have to give it back. You can even ask."

Now the woman wasn't smiling at all. She took off her sunglasses and dropped them into the bag.

"Why give it back? You take the money and I'll take the doll. It'll be our little secret." She smiled again, bigger this time. "We'll leave those other people out of it."

Pip didn't wait to hear any more. He darted around the woman and raced toward the cliffs.

9

Pip ran as fast as he could along the cliff toward his house. Once he fell and scraped his knee. He got up and checked to make sure he still had both dolls. Then he sprinted the last few hundred yards.

Seconds later he banged through the kitchen door. He heard his mother's voice. "Mike? Is that you?"

Pip hadn't caught his breath yet. He went to the sink and gulped some water.

His mother came into the kitchen. "Pip, what happened to you? Your clothes are filthy and your hair is full of cobwebs! What have you and Davey been doing?"

"Mom, I've got to talk to you and Dad. It's important!"

"Daddy is shopping, and don't change the subject, young man. Why do you look like you've been playing in a sewer? And where's your rain slicker?"

"I was under Davey's porch. Mom, this lady is after me. She wants my doll and she stole my backpack and I think she snuck into my room!"

"Please slow down, Pip. Your knee is bleeding!" She made him sit down. "How did this happen? Brad Ramsey, what have you been up to?"

"Mom, I'm trying to tell you! Some lady is following me. She wants the doll!"

"What lady?" Pip's father came through the back door carrying a bag of groceries. "Pip, have you been cleaning the basement with your hair?"

Pip's mother wet a paper towel and wiped his knee. She pulled some of the cobwebs from his hair. "I think you have something to tell us," she said.

"That's what I'm trying to do, Mom!"

"Can we all stay calm?" his father said. "Okay, Pip. Take a few breaths and tell us what's going on."

Pip started with the phone call he received the day after the yard sale.

"Why weren't we informed of this phone call?" his mother demanded, smoothing a Band-Aid onto his knee.

"I told you about it," Pip said. "You didn't listen. Nobody listens around here!"

"Go on with your story," his father said. "We're listening."

Pip told his parents how he thought Matt's mother hadn't been telling the truth the night before. "I was there when Matt's father gave him the doll to sell. It was in a box of stuff. So Matt's mother was lying, wasn't she?"

His parents looked at each other, then back at Pip.

"Davey and I rode over to Matt's house to find out what was going on. Matt told us his father got a phone call, too. Someone offered him two hundred dollars!"

"Time out, Pipper," his father said. "Are you saying that someone offered you both money for this doll?"

Pip nodded. "And today she followed me to Davey's house and tried to buy the doll. I recognized her voice from the telephone. That's why I ran back here."

"Tell us about this lady, please," Pip's mother said.

"I don't know who she is. She said she was at the yard sale."

"There must have been a dozen people there," his mother said. "What does she look like?"

Pip closed his eyes for a second. "She's real tall, like Dad. She's got yellow hair and she was wearing one of those shiny black raincoats."

"I remember her!" Pip's mother said. "She introduced herself. Her name is Cora Winters. She teaches Russian history at the college."

"And this woman actually tried to buy

the doll from you?" Pip's father said.

Pip nodded. "She says she wants the doll because she collects stuff from Russia."

"Well, this is the strangest thing I've ever heard," said Pip's mother. "If the woman wants this doll so much, why didn't she just come over here and talk to us?"

"I have a feeling she thought she could get a better deal from our Pip," his father said. "I think she wanted to avoid his parents."

"Where's the doll now, Pip?" his mother asked.

Pip told his parents that Jason had run off with the smallest doll, and then his backpack had disappeared with the other two dolls in it.

"But I got them all back," he said. He pulled two of the dolls out of his pockets. "The other one's at Davey's. I hid it under his bed."

Pip's mother picked up the smallest doll. "This poor guy looks a little beat up," she said. "What happened to him?"

"Davey's dog must have chewed on it before he buried it," Pip said. "Do I really have to give the doll back, Dad?"

"Well, you agreed to try and find the dolls for Matt's mother, remember? If this Cora Winters is really willing to pay two hundred dollars, the money should go to them."

"Is there a fourth boy inside this little one?" Pip's mother asked.

Pip shook his head. "Davey and I tried to take it apart. There's no opening."

"Well, there is now. Look."

Pip leaned across the table. Where Jason's teeth had punctured the wood, some paint had chipped away. Pip now saw a thin crack around the boy's waist.

Pip's mother pulled a knife out of the table drawer. She forced the blade into the crack. Specks of paint fell onto the table. She twisted the knife and the doll came apart with a soft pop.

A mound of brown cloth stuck out of the bottom half of the doll. The cloth was wrapped around something. Pip pulled the lump out and unwrapped the cloth.

A second later he held a strange object in his hand. The sunlight coming through the kitchen window made it sparkle like a million tiny stars.

"Oh, my," Pip's mother whispered. "Oh, my goodness gracious."

10

Pip stared at the thing in his hand. "What is it?"

"Honey, put it down, will you?" his father said. "Set it on the cloth. Gently, Pip."

"Is that what I think it is?" Pip's mother asked.

"A Fabergé egg," her husband said.

Pip asked, "What's a whatever-you-said egg?"

The object they were all staring at was the size and shape of a duck egg. It stood on a gold pedestal that was covered with diamonds. The shell part of the egg was decorated with small golden eagles. The eagles' feathers were made of hundreds of tiny diamonds. Their eyes were emeralds and their feet and legs were rubies.

"The Russian czars used to give Easter gifts to their wives back in the 1800s," Pip's father explained. "One of the czars asked a jeweler named Carl Fabergé to make something special for his wife. He made a fabulous jeweled egg, and the czarina loved it. Fabergé turned out a bunch of these over the years. Each new egg was different."

"The eggs open up," Pip's mother said. "Fabergé put a surprise inside, like a gold object or a jewel."

"Let's open this one!" Pip reached for the egg, but his father stopped his hand.

"Pip, this is worth a lot of money. It's old and very fragile." He picked up the knife and used it as a pointer. "See, here's the latch that opens the egg."

"But how did this egg thingie get inside my doll?"

"You remember Matt's mom telling us the doll once belonged to her husband's great-aunt?" Pip's father said. "She brought it here from Russia when she was a little girl."

Pip's mother nodded. "And this has been hidden inside the doll for nearly eighty years. Until Pip Ramsey bought it with my dollar bill!"

"But why did they put the egg in the doll?" Pip asked.

"Someone probably wanted to sneak the egg out of Russia," his father said. "There was a war going on. People were starving to death. Who knows how the aunt's family ever got hold of the egg in the first place."

Pip's mother slid the egg closer. "I can't believe a Fabergé egg is standing on our kitchen table."

"So what do we do with it?" Pip asked. "Is it mine?"

Pip's father took a five-dollar bill out of his wallet. "Pretend I gave this to you. You put it in your coat pocket and forgot all about it. Then you gave the coat to Davey. Who do you think should get the five bucks, you or Davey?"

"Me!"

"Right. So who do you think should get the egg?"

"Matt?"

"Well, the doll was in Matt's family," his father said. "So they have first dibs on the egg."

Pip stroked the top of the egg. "Will Matt be rich?"

His father smiled. "Very rich, Pip."

"I don't know about you guys," Pip's mother said. "But I'm a little nervous with a priceless egg in the house."

"Let's take it over to Matt's," Pip suggested. "Hey, now they won't have to sell their farm, will they?"

His father laughed. "Pipper, they can buy a dozen farms with what this little egg is worth."

"That's why that woman wants the doll, right?"

Pip's parents looked at each other over the egg. "She must have known the egg was in that doll," his mother said.

"Yeah, so she stole my backpack and broke into my room! Let's call the cops!"

"Hold it, Pip," his father said. "We have no proof this woman did anything other than offer to buy the doll."

"The rest is conjecture, Pip," his mother said.

"What's that?"

"It means we're just guessing that she did those other things."

Pip put the two dolls together and stood them up. "But don't you want to find out? Then we'll know for sure if she was snooping in our house."

His father carefully rewrapped the Fabergé egg in its cloth. "And how do we find out, Pip?"

Pip grinned. "Simple. Let's call her up and invite her over."

There was a C. Winters listed in the Ogunquit phone book. Pip's mother made the call. She told Mrs. Winters that her son had bought an old wooden doll at a yard sale. She asked if Mrs. Winters would come and look at the doll.

"It looks Russian, and I remember that you teach Russian history. We'd like to know if the doll is worth anything," Pip's mother said into the phone. "We might be interested in selling the doll."

Pip's mother hung up. "Cora Winters will be here in an hour," she said.

11

Pip, Davey, and Mike hid in the kitchen. When Mrs. Winters showed up, they could hear her voice through the door.

"She sure talks loud," Mike whispered.

Pip tried to picture her in his bedroom, poking through his dinosaurs and books, searching for the doll.

Davey had brought his pack over, so now Pip had all three dolls back together again. He walked into the living room and handed the doll to his father.

Mrs. Winters looked at Pip. "Hello, there," she said.

Pip looked at his sneakers. He felt too

embarrassed to look at Mrs. Winters.

"Isn't this fun?" she said. "I just love those wooden nesting dolls! Finding one from before the Russian Revolution is such a happy accident!"

Happy accident my foot, Pip thought. *You've been trying to steal it from me!*

Pip's father gave the doll to Mrs. Winters.

"Do you think it's worth anything?" Pip's mother asked.

"I'm willing to write you a check for one hundred dollars right now," Mrs. Winters said. She was smiling as she reached into her bag and took out a checkbook.

Pip's mother glanced at him and nodded. Pip walked over to the fireplace. He took the Fabergé egg off the mantel. It had been in plain sight the whole time.

His voice felt shaky. He had rehearsed what he was going to say, but he was still nervous.

"We found this inside the littlest doll," he told Mrs. Winters. He showed her the egg.

"Is the doll still worth a hundred dollars

to you?" his father asked. "Without the egg inside?"

Mrs. Winters lost her smile. She hadn't moved an inch since Pip took the egg down from the mantel. Suddenly she threw the wooden doll to the floor.

"You knew!" she yelled. "You people invited me over here and you knew!"

"No, Mrs. Winters," Pip's father said softly. "*You* knew. Somehow you learned what was inside the doll. You tried to get your hands on it by any means. You offered my son money over the telephone. When he refused your offer, I believe you stole his backpack and broke into our home. All the time, you knew the egg was inside the doll."

For a minute Mrs. Winters didn't say anything. She glared at Pip's father with fire shooting from her eyes.

Then she shrugged. "I teach Russian history. When I read about the yard sale, I decided to go. The ad in the paper said Russian books would be for sale. I found an old diary and bought it. I read the diary that evening. One entry said that a czarina's egg was hidden in their daughter's wooden doll. She was coming to the United States, and the doll would come with her."

Mrs. Winters looked over at Pip. "I remembered seeing you buy the doll. I assumed—correctly, as it turns out—that the diary and the doll belonged to the same family years ago."

Pip stared at the toes of his sneakers. No one said anything. The clock in the corner sounded a lot louder than it usually did.

Mrs. Winters left the room without saying another word.

Pip jumped when the front door slammed. A few seconds later he heard a car roar out of the driveway. He felt embarrassed, but he wasn't sure why. He was sorry for Mrs. Winters, and that puzzled him, too.

Davey picked up the doll. Pip took it apart and put the egg back inside the smallest one. Then he stood the three dolls on the mantel.

"Now what?" Mike asked.

"Now we call Matt and tell him he's rich!" Pip said.

"Let's keep that as a surprise," Pip's mother suggested. "Why not just call Matt's parents and tell them you found the doll?"

Fifteen minutes later a truck pulled into the driveway. Pip, Davey, and Mike ran out to the porch.

Pip stared when Matt's family climbed out of the truck. He counted four little girls, all carrying coloring books and boxes of crayons.

Matt's mother herded the kids toward the house. Pip's parents invited everyone into the living room, and Mike poured lemonade and passed cookies.

Pip took the smallest doll off the mantel and handed it to Matt. "Pull it open," he said.

Matt pulled the top off. Everyone stared at the egg, shining out of the dull wood.

"What's that?" Matt's father asked.

"It's an imperial Fabergé egg," Pip's father said. "It's been inside that old doll since it left Russia, Mr. Donavich."

Pip's father explained how Fabergé had made the eggs for the Russian czars' wives. "There were fifty or so eggs made," he explained. "Some are in museums and private collections. A few have never been found, and one of those was inside the doll."

Matt's parents stared at the egg.

"Excuse me," Matt's mother said. "Is this egg worth any money?"

"Only about a million dollars, more or less," Pip's father said.

Pip thought Matt's mother was going to start crying.

Her husband's mouth dropped open.

Matt stuffed a whole cookie into his mouth.

"Now you won't have to sell your farm and move," Pip said.

"You're giving the egg to us?" Matt's mother said.

"It belongs to you," Pip's mother said. "The egg was in your aunt's doll all these years."

Matt's mother shook her head. "But your son bought the doll. It's his now."

Everyone looked at Pip.

"I only wanted the doll," he said. "You guys can have the egg."

Matt handed the doll with the egg inside to his mother. She took the egg out and passed it to her husband. Mr. Donavich took out his handkerchief and wrapped it around the egg. "I break things easily," he said.

Everyone laughed. Pip fitted the two smaller dolls into the largest one and stood it on the fireplace mantel.

The wooden farmer boy smiled at all the people in the room, as if he knew a secret.

About the Author

RON ROY has written more than twenty books for children. Though he lives in Connecticut, he often visits Ogunquit, Maine, the town where this book is set. Ron says he has found many priceless treasures there...including the idea for this story.

About the Illustrator

ELIZABETH WOLF lives in Boise, Idaho, with her husband, her two children, and her dog, June, who happily posed as Jason. Elizabeth has illustrated many children's books.